T0062767

When It Comes to Real Love

Sheremirah Jones

Order this book online at www.trafford.com
or email orders@trafford.com

Most Trafford titles are also available at major online book retailers.

© Copyright 2011 Sheremirah Jones.
All rights reserved. No part of this publication may be reproduced, stored in a retrieval
system, or transmitted, in any form or by any means, electronic, mechanical, photocopying,
recording, or otherwise, without the written prior permission of the author.

Printed in the United States of America.

ISBN: 978-1-4269-6570-8 (sc)
ISBN: 978-1-4269-6939-3 (hc)
ISBN: 978-1-4269-6571-5 (e)

Library of Congress Control Number: 2011907541

Trafford rev. 05/11/2011

www.trafford.com

North America & international
toll-free: 1 888 232 4444 (USA & Canada)
phone: 250 383 6864 ✦ fax: 812 355 4082

I love to love you

I love to love you. I love that you're with me.
Near me and all over me.
I love when you're in me. Just to caress
You're necked back. As you go up and down inside
Of me. I lose control. I'm in another world I
Love what you do to me. Even though I don't
Know what it is. But I know I don't want
You to quit. I love to love you. It's easy and
Fun. The sex is so great it feels like I am
In another place. But safe in our own place.
I love to love you. I want you on top of me.
Colide with me slide if you please. Show me
that you're loving me. Study me as
You rub me. Give it to me this and that way.
Push it inside of me and caress me. Sometimes
Try to undress me.

But Him

The one I love
And think of.
Want no one.
But when will he come.
I love him.
Love him and only him.
Hard to realize.
Created in this world to feel.
To live maybe even steal.
To continue forever and ever.
Caring a torch for someone.
Run with it until the end of time.
If my love is real then the fire will stay still.
Because in my heart there nothing but love for him.

He Doesn't Know

He doesn't know that my love will take care of him
For life. He doesn't know that it's going to be hard
For me to walk away. Even if my true feelings won't
Let me stay. He doesn't know that I know how deeply
Hurt he is sometimes. He doesn't know that his eyes
Say it all. The hurt behind all the jokes and the pretty
Brown eyes and wonderful smile. He doesn't know
That I will be by his side. Where ever and whenever.
I wouldn't and couldn't just walk away from something
That feels and sixty five days of knowing someone.
He doesn't know that my love will go where he goes.

I Need To Be

I need to be where the beautiful things are.
Where flowers flow and water ripples.

Where old plan leaves catch the wind breeze.
Where everything is quiet and at a stand still.
I need to be there is meditation.

I need to be where things feel alive.
Where things talk but don't actually have lips.
But you can just vibe there conversation is happening.

A place where love is so strong it's what you look like.
This place is a feel good place.
A restrain from all evil.

𝓗𝓔

He jabs and he jabs; He thrust and he thrust.
As he bust and he bust.
As he pounds and he pounds; up and down up and down.
Round and round; nothing but sounds nothing but sounds.
All around, all around.
As he clowns and he clowns.
He thinks he's clowning while he's going up and downing.
Talking the talk trying to make some sparks.
So later you can't walk the walk.
Because he'll talk the talk.
So you can't forget that he hit.
Because he has a stick, a stick.
He thinks he's the shit the shit.
He won't quit he won't quit.
Until you admit you admit.
That he's the shit, the shit.

The Calm Confidence

Come inside my mind and with your lust you will find.
A little piece and time.
To decline and maybe be mine.
Cool and smooth almost like a baby's move.
Pull to the top never try and stop.
Find your way then you can stay.
You may need to lay on the bay, try to see the day.
Cry don't sigh.
Try and be fly I'll tell you why, you'll feel high.
Its life that makes you feel tight.
Like the midnight sight.

Will He

Will he come to me?
And haunt me.
Like a dream.
When I scream.
Will he ever be there with open arms?
What will he look like?
Is it emotions?
Will he shine like a token?
Will he be open?
Will he ever come clean?
And show me he's not mean.
Is he going to be totally there for me?
Not willing to share me.
Will it ever come a day that I will find my way.
Is he going to keep hiding from what's inside?

Birth

The day that we prey has finally come today.
I came out in sight.
To finally see the light.
The next day I stay with a woman.
Who said she knew I was coming.
A few days past, it was a week at last.
A year has passed; I began to crawl real fast.
Everyone see's me so unique.
I feel tall and strong and I feel like I have a home.

I Remember

I remember the caress of your hand.
You're who I want to call my man.
I remember the touch of your finger tips.
As I imagine them as your lips.
I remember your stroke up and down my spine.
You declined, oh so fine
I felt like you where really mine.
The rapture of your arms, kept me safe from harm.
The safe feeling.
That was so appealing.

This Moment for Life

Wish I could have this moment for life.
Right in the moment so good so desirable.
Maybe the way the wind felt on my cheek, as
I felt your embrace that I so longed for.

The smile on a child's face that's wowed by
Having his father.
The warmth of his love, he's as lovely as a dove.
A moment of hunger in his eyes.

Reading them reading he.
Telling her she is lovely.
The night brings so many things.
Vampire acts the feeling is in you.

You feel like two.
The time takes over the day time you.
Night time moments are like life time moments.
Animal reactions dogs chase the cats.
Cats looking back just ready to attack.

LOVE

When times are hard love is lord.
Heart is lonely and alone.
Crying want to cry.
Love your kids.
Remince on when.
Love so much.
No one understands where's the man?
Does he take a stand?

Love when you can.
Suppose to love you.
Never lower myself, love for you.
Just to be within in, maybe within him.
Don't worry for consequences.

Love is me and everyone real around me.
Trying to get every he to indulged me.

Your sexy and tempting full of lust.
Have your way of having your way.
Strong mind getting into mine.
One look and I'm hooked.
You say do, I say "no."
But end up not being able to say no.
I love your appeal.
Satisfies my sexual appetite.
You handle me smooth and tuff, but just enough to "bust."
Lust all over the room, when you enter and meet eyes with mine.
From your head to toe is where I'd like to go.
Your hands on me and your body touching up against me.
Feeds me like a plate of steak.
With all my might I wonder.
Why does your thunderstorm down for me.
I don't neglect it, just be right there to be wet in it.

I Can't Believe It

Every voice in my head won't let me believe it.
Believe that I'm here.
I'm here lying down with you.
Quiet, nice, and peaceful.
Rubbing your chest.
Falling asleep at your heartbeat.
Sun shinning through your window on us.
After so long I'm proud to have you back in my arms again.
Glad to call you "mine" again.
Glad to walk through your door.
And into your arms.
Glad to see my sunshine.
My everything.
My reason for living.
The great thing I have that other girls don't.
My wonderful smile.
Happy to love me because I love him.
Tells me I am his greatest thing.

My Wedding Vows to "The"

I was offered a proposal.
Which I already had my answer.
He wants me to marry him.
He's wealthy, he has everything to offer.
My answer,
I will marry the for love.
I will marry you to cherish you.
I will take the hand, so you can forever remain my man.
And that be my reason to marry the.
So I can always have he, beneath me between our bed sheets.
To wake up to your warm chest against my breast.
To think all the rest don't have the best.
To finally exhale and feel so well.
To be glad and not sad, I will marry the.

Our Life

Our life was so tight I thought I'd be your wife.
Our long nights without fights. Always felt so right.
We started a family. I thought you where the man for me.
I came into an ok family. With a man I thought needed
Me. But now my life is intact. Because the man that holds my
hand, is my one and a true fan. He's mine and only
Mine. He's fine like wine. Shine's like a dime. Does for his love.
He's the one now I'm free like a bee, to do me with he. We don't
fuss and fight. Or argue every night he's alright maybe the love
of my life.

Without

Without he.
Without thought.
Without fault.
Without touch.
Without speak.
Without words.
Just without he.
Makes this hole
Thing absurd.
Without answers.
Without help.
Without a babies
    Father.
Without my love.
Without his sex.
 Without our next.
Without next.
Without the best.
Without everything
Being set.
Me going hand and hand with he.
I love the; and I
Miss dearly.
My love for him will
    Forever be.
I love this man.

A Virgo Me

A Virgo me. I found a Virgo me.
One who acts and talks and thinks like me.
They say opposites attract but still I've found a match.
And now I'm real attached.
Then the sex was the best.
Both of us rubbing chest to chest.
We felt like forgetting all the rest.
Passing passion through the air.
Feeling was like I'd been there before.
Maybe this right shouldn't of happened, but the
Fight wasn't with me.
A Virgo me.

Love Is.............

Whispering I love you's in the middle of the night.
Love is......
Awakening with him on your mind.
Love is......
The years you've shared together.
Love is......
Thoughts of your marriage.
Love is......
A baby that looks just like him.
Love is......
Helping him get on his feet.
Love is......
Taking him in when he's sick.
Love is......
Following him to the edge of the world.
Love is......
My one and true fantasy!
     I love you

Relaxation

Soft talks under the light, sparkle bright.
It feels so right, we watch the night.
And love the sight.
Eyes so bright and a lovely white.
Peel the dark , and feel a spark.
Stretch your arch, as you began to start.
Lay on your back; feels so flat.
Close your eyes.
And relax your thighs.
Never sigh just feel alive.

As The Fire Place Burns

As the fire place wood burns;
The fire inside me yearns.
For more than I can adore
Like my man holding my hand.
Walking me through the sand.
The man that's my life and the reason
Why I fight.
My reason for trying to
Exist, are things like his kiss.
That perfect life in which;
Id be his wife.
Wanting to hold it together,
And feeling like being apart,
Would be never.
You try and think without he you
Could still be a family.
The thought of that is like a story
With no ending.
Have you ever loved a he and just wished
He'd just believe in the.
A real love like no other does really exist.
It starts with a kiss.
As the fireplace burns.

The Girl

Sweet bitter sorrows run through her head.
Black clouds cover her sky.
Sadness runs threw her eyes.
Two holes are poked through her soul.
Weird thoughts about lovers.
Two people running crazy thoughts through her mind.
She said she is happy she is weary then back to sad.
Sometimes hard decisions feel her mined.
She doesn't know what to choose from
Him or him.
He loves her, he loves her too.
She loves him kind of loves the other.
Doesn't no what to choose from.
She had fallen in love and it was oh so great.
She knew he loved her too.
As they got older, the love started to change
Who was this man?
What happened to my lover, I fell in love with.
Why is he doing this to me?
How are we going to make this work?
They couldn't find the answer so they fell apart.

The Long Kiss Goodbye!

The love that they thought they had.
to put there hands out and to have someone
at the end of your reach.
Was just so sweet.
But now why the long kiss goodbye.
It was a delight; but now
    They fight.
They were together for years.
Until she began to shed tears.
Now every moment ends with a sad goodbye.
A hand shake but no hug.
Or all; it's not going to work.
We can still be friends.
And when you least exspect your hole world comes falling down.
       You ask why
     But they have no reason.
       You are alone now.

Things You Can Be For Me

You can be my light bulb; and brighten up my day.
You can be my strength; and help me be strong.
You can be my sun; and be there in the morning.
You can be my bed; and I'll sleep all over you.
You can be my car; and drive me wherever I need to go.
But there is some things I don't want you to be.......
I don't want you to be a light switch I don't want to turn you
On and off.
I don't want you to be a recorder,
I don't want to here things over and over.
I don't want you to be a tick; don't want you up under me
All the time.
I don't want you to be a pest.
I don't want to be bothered.
So all I'm saying is be my man.
Don't irritate me, love me, don't be under me all the time.
Just be there for me, and be good to me.

A Dose of Love

I walked up to he.
Clutched his hands.
Looked into his eyes.
Felt his presents.
And his body next to the.
I ran my hands up his arms.
Up to his shoulder.
Stopping at his neck.
Slowly resting my palms.
A beautiful swan.
Is what I felt like.
How tight the night stars are.
Far in the dark.
In the misty blue dark.
We stand hand and hand.
Feeling all over this man.
A small virgin drugged from your love.
In her pupils a picture of he.
Unique because she can't speak.
Enhanced in a trance.
Filled with nothing but romance.
Anytime she feels the need for wine.
He doses her with love.
And most of her feels like a pearl.

Suddenly

The instinct.
The unexpected.
The time for all talking to cease.
The one person you call.
A friend always there to the end.
          Unexpected.
But you have to let this.
If you don't then you'll regret it.
Many, many times all up in your face, he shined.
You gave him nothing but time.
As he tried to get into your mind.
Looking for true love.
Well God sent it down from up above.

His Presents

Knocked up against the wall.
Never to fall.
Just stalled and appalled
A burst of your desert.
All underneath my skirt.
He flirts underneath my skirt.
Not seen but still he clinged.
All over me is were his hands went.
Where is the, in front of me?
Good with his hands.
Putting me in a trance.
Taking my romance.
And turned it into intense feelings.
Where is he?
I want to feel the.
Just as much as I want to appease the.
Come into thy sight.
Let me feel your silk skin.
Come within me and be friend me.

Passion

Urgently desiring possessions.
Greedy giving pleasure and satisfaction,
With my body actions.
I will snatch and take you suddenly.
I will perceive you through the sense of touch.
"It's hot"
A violently burst of steam.
Seize and hold me tightly.
The extreme warmth of my passion is exploding from within.
Give in take a spin.
Come clean and don't be mean.
I have seen your intense attraction.
Your longing desire.
It's a craving, if I'm not mistaking.
I am propelling to you.
Do I attract you with entice reward that it brings great pleasure
To you.

Doesn't He Know it's over

Does he know it's over?
Still he chooses to hover.
Like a cover.
He wants a kiss.
But that is something that I can not miss.
He looks and romances.
As he wishes, to give me kisses
Doesn't he know it's over?
He played around; and never frowned.
While I stood my grown; and wore a crown.
I didn't share; a blissful glare.
I did my hair; and stood aware.
I gave a shove; hoping he'd show his love.

Lonely Heart

Sneak around.
And follow the ground, far out of town.
To fool around.
As lovely as it sounds.
You leave your frown.
You're on your own.
No need to moan.
Listen to the tone.
You don't need to feel alone.
Just find a phone.
And call up everyone at home.
Follow that smell.
That smell that smells so well.
Go to the hotel door.
Walk in and look at the floor.
You won't be looking so poor.
You'll feel some glory once more.
As you see everyone, you adore.

I Have A Secret!

I feel a sensation.
A perfect creation.
Of an image once taken.
And me and he.
Underneath bed sheets.
I get weak.
It's something I'm wanting.
Something that he's flaunting.
Never had intercourse.
But maybe it's mint for us.
Filled with lust.
A hush comes over me.
Then I to see why.
I feel so high.
It's thrown at me.
But perfection I do not see.
Can I go with he?
And be free.
And have a treat.

Virgin 2K

Virgin 2K is a virgin today.
Lonely as I lay; but a virgin I will stay.
Standing on the bay; looking at the day.
Century 2 has now become you.
Through and through your never blue.
Because inside you're deeply moved.
At how long it took for you;
to keep what was really true.

Good People

Good people are the neglected.
Evil lives like an illness.
Good is the cure but no one wants to take it.
Just want to destroy it and tear it down.
Like people do your feelings as if you don't have them.

You smile they smile but above there heads are horns or evil.
But the good in the good just won't let us see that.
We're being attacked everyday fighting and fighting trying to be
Strong for another day. You don't have to deal with us.

I See His Struggle

I love me love my family.
We just want to be free.
The he that means a lot to me.
Struggles a lot for he.
We want we hunt.
Try and try to have what we want and need.

He is a good man, one no one can stand.
I write about he because I see the eyes in he.
What's there struggle.

No one is of his struggle.
They don't know of what pain he became.
And what opposite sex brought him some mess.
Never letting him rest.
I see the struggle in his eyes.

Good man always holding you by the hand if he can
Woman man always saying, "I CAN" He is the man.
SEDD

Going Crazy

Going crazy missing you like this. Don't know what to do. You should have never been my "who." What am I suppose to do about the fact that I want you. The thoughts in my mine; are wondering around sooner or later they may make it to my heart but I'm hoping they'll wonder apart. Long as I 'm here without you, I constantly want you. I wonder what you've done to me like you like you wonder what I've done to you. We've just become "Me" and "He" constantly wanting she and wanting he. But is it we me, my mind personality my common ideas. Or since of having things in common. The look in your eye that's so sexy, but sneaky and a little freaky. Makes me let you have all control. To have and appeal as strong as yours. Makes me want you more.

Cry!

Sometimes things hurt so bad you can't even cry.
You can't feel the tear in the bottom of our eye.
Men lie you wonder why.
You just want stay high.
Maybe even fly and feel the sky.
You know you need to cry or just release someone from your life.
Just get the devil from behind the.
Follow he the one who gives his self to she instead of me.
Cry, cry, cry, cry.
Water down the eye.
Doesn't solve anything.
But new things can be seen.

Pray.......................

Pray for change in my life, and a rearrange in my life.
Something's aren't to be.
Like me and he, and especially she.
They have a family.
But the man is always with me.
Pray for all the bad things to be pushed away from me.
I don't want he like some might think of me.
My two are my crew.
He can go, she can go.
I have his baby and that is driving me crazy.
Whatever is sad, things are not good and stressful.
I wouldn't give a dame about a man.
I don't need no one holding my hand.
Even the good feeling of the love I carry for he.

How Can You Go Back

How can you go back from what we did.
We put two together and became something we thought we could remain.
Friends when we began we thought it was until the end.
Feelings got involved.
My love had to fall.
How can you go back?
Thought I had found my mountain, I was ready to climb you.
You can't go back from good lovemaking.
Thigh kissing gentle touch.
Shower sex being picked up to never fall.
Washing you, you washing me; looking at you, you looking at me.

When We Feel Each Other
We Melt Within each other.

The last time we felt each other we melted within each other.
Inside, and out our passion, was so relaxing.
The touch of memory.
The lust within us.
It's not a crush but of so much more.
Not yet, love, but sex sure does carry us up above.
This could turn into love.
I feel like I've been stung by a bug.
every time we touch, our love seems to combust.
When I see, you I just want to eat you.
Kiss all over your soft big lips.
I see you talking but I can't here you.
I can only feel your lips against mine.
Soft and supal.
Every time we see each other our love melts within each other.

Things Have Changed

Things have changed they didn't have to remain the same. Don't know what the deal is, are where he is. Doing new things, to be unseen. It's a new year, came through it with no fear. So far, I'm not doing the same thing. Maybe thinking of the same man. Truth be told he was last year. And we went through that with a cheer and a tear because no one was near. Being alone is my only fear. But since the New Year is here, I'm going to start something different had planned all along. Sing a new song about my life my fight. My struggle my hustle and my trouble. Came into something new and trying to leave the old behind. But as soon as you see, a face seems like all gets erased. Can't believe how some people can change on you. If you are going to do something new, why leave everybody without a clue. Suppose to be loyal to the end, if that's already how you've began. Leaving people in the wind, and then you try to come back and pick up where you left off. Guess what they will have started new friendships, relationships that don't include you. So go back to where you were at because evidently that's where you should be since it was never about me. Need to know how to now ones mind who never tells you what is in there eyes.

Love Hurts

Love hurts in such a strong way.
I walk upon his present's everyday.
Soft thoughts through my mined about he.
But how could I have he, when I already have the.
But, when he speaks, I get weak
Lovely and neat, pretty to his feet.
I take a peek, everyday and every way.
I stay away don't want him afraid.
But still I prey.
Maybe some day we would be as one.
I see my equal, but he loves playing games with me.
I have a man but at the same time, I want your hand.
So sweet and unique.

I don't know what to do without you.
I see my soul mate, and every sweet date.
I am what you need.
I can be all you need if you let me.
I feel as if you have a good thing right in front of you.
But you don't notice me.
You're going to let me slip right through your fingers like silk.
I carry a very phenomenon lust for you.
A very respectful lust.
You deserve a lot and I am willing to give it to you.
I hurt when I see your pretty smile.
But it's not aimed at me.
My smile falls to see you wrap your arm around her.

I don't have any of your acknowledgements.
Can I get some of your conversation you share so well?

If you were mine, I'd wrap you up like a present.
And treat you delicate like glass.
Treat you precious like diamonds.
All I want is your affection.
It's hard to realize what you want.
Its hard to stay and feel so gray.
I gaze at you a lot and wish that you were mine.
You're a 1st prize I'd like to win.
When I'd walk with you on my arm. I'd feel like the luckiest girl
In the world.
Because I'd have a pearl in my world.

How you got inside my mind and now time is like wine, just fine.
Someone had me before you but just as strong.
But your love is lasting longer; you make me hunger.
What type of thunder did you roll under?
Under my feet that made me so weak.
Seek, seek the we that made our lust.
The lust that bust through and made a new you.
Who I became to love as I slide away from the.
But the time he returns to my presents my body is not rejecting.
It's just steady letting me love him; and feel his love.
He passes through me anytime we touch.
I love this man and I would LOVE to have his hand.
I already had his little man.
This man stays in my mind as well as in my heart.
I run to the end of the earth with he.
No one understands me
They don't understand my love nor do I care or want them to.
His is I and he is we.
Virgo.

When you rise inside.
I collide and slide, like ice.
You make me feel so right.
You're my baby. I love to
Hear your name. It keeps
Me from going insane.
Just to sit and speak your
Name. My love for you will
Forever remain. When you
Touch me it makes me want
To always, rush to you.
I am filled with lust for you.
I'm in a hush when you,
Put that stuff in me.
Like a chill to me. Like ice
Cold you put out my fire.
And that rocks me to sleep.
And makes me weak.
But keeps me feeling like
Mink. I write my love across
The sky for you. I will
Never deny you. This is a
Feeling of every girls wish.
For a man like you to place a
Kiss upon once lips. I have a Jones
For you. That makes me flaunt you.
You don't know what you've
done to me. In my mind you're
constantly
The one for me. Going out of your

To see that beautiful face
Makes a heart race.
Filled up to never be let
down. Your love is so
good. As it should go on
And on. Like an endless
song. Like and endless
that you sing to me but
you mean the words.
That makes me fly like a
Bird. So many words I've
Heard from you. Never
to sound up surd. Famous
For smiling and brightening
up one's day. Making up
Love stories. Taking love
To another level. Making
Love for a reason. Making
it all the more exciting.
trying to take two in order
to make a new "You."
keeping a clue to who you
Want to stay true to.
Loving the way my female
path feels. To you It's a
Great appeal. You never
seem to neglect a bit.
Like my intelligence

and my sex appeal.

Way to save the day. You should
Be my hero. I'm always waiting to
See when you will come to me.
Float on our own cloud
Nine. Pretending there's
No one around. No sounds
And no frowns. And we're
All around. We've escaped the
Fast pace race of trying to
Get somewhere. Because
Now we are there. And we are
Not going no where. Because I'm
Here and you're here. So we're
Both near. Standing here with
The same fear. And that would
Be to be lonely. Since we finally
Together forever we feel as if we
Are each others love treasure.
Never to be disturbed so now we
Can here each others words.
We can look into each others eyes.
Hold hands and walk among
The sand. Feel the romance from
Everyone as we watch them glance.
Now we have a chance to feel like
We're in a dream. Having nothing
Came between the things that love
Means. All the thoughts that our
Love could crash are now In the passed.
Now we realize our love did last.

I think these things
give you a real thrill.
We will constantly

He Is Within Me.

He is within me.
The sex was me and he
Between the sheets.
Doing it like we've
Known each other forever.
Felt like birds were
Dropping love feathers.
It was like it was
Something we'd waited so
Long for. He held me in his
I felt this man within
Myself. Now every time
He holds me I melt.
The look in his eyes
Gives me a real high.
Shoots up my spine.
He knows how to look
At me; and put his hooks
In me.
He keeps me wanting he
He is within me.

21st Century

It was the 21st century and a sparkle burst within me.
I saw a face, in a beautiful place.
It smiled at me and wild me.
This face was full of grace.
It put me In space.
After meeting this face we began to relate.
Mind to mind; soon this face was mine.
It was he for me.
I love every look; lips with the right hook.
Smile stands out in a crowd.
Skin is something you'd love to win.
A flawless face you'd love looking at; across
At it on a date.
It's a lovely sleeping face.
A reach over and softly kiss at night face.
A big face, but more to love.
My 21st Century love me some he.

Something Toke Hold Of Me

My breath has been taken away.
There's not a thought in my mind; as I watch out the
Window at the sunshine.
Not a memory a dream nor a daydream came to me.
What can this be.
Me.
Without a thought of he.
Knowing I am very lonely.
Something just toke hold of me.
And it wants me to see.
Maybe relax and just be me.
Get away from my usual day.
Stay in the gray and not in black or white.
Something held me tight and made me feel alright.
I want this again; but at night.
With the man I call my life who wants me to be his wife.
And stay forever in his sight each and every night.
That one man who is my light.
Something toke a hold of me, and held me tight.
I love you.......................

Printed in the United States
By Bookmasters